WKRISHIND
Nature's Creation

KARYALA

Dr. Monika Shandil

Wkrishind Publishers
WKRISHIND.IN
Edition: I

Dr. Monika Shandil
Shimla, H.P.
WKRISHIND.IN

Acknowledgement

Expression of feeling by words makes them less significant when it comes to expressing gratitude. However, I would like to take this opportunity to express my deepest appreciation and gratitude to everyone who has contributed to the completion of this book.

First and foremost, I am immensely thankful to the almighty for granting me countless blessings and opportunities throughout this journey. Their divine guidance and support have been instrumental in my accomplishments.

I would like to extend my heartfelt gratitude to my guide, Professor Shashi Kant, for his unwavering support. I would also like to express my sincere appreciation to all the **Karyala** artists who generously dedicated their precious time to the interviews. Their willingness to share their experiences and perspectives has added depth and richness to this book.

Last but not least, I want to acknowledge the unwavering support and inspiration provided by my parents. They have been my pillars of strength throughout this journey, and I am forever grateful for their love, encouragement, and unwavering belief in me. I would also like to express my gratitude to all those who have accompanied me on this journey.

Contents

Chapter -1

Introduction

Folk theatre, as a mode of communication, is a composite art form in India, with a fusion of elements from music, dance, pantomime, versification, epic, and cultural performances embedded in local areas. Himachal Pradesh, known as the land of deities, incorporates folk performances into every festival, fair ceremony, or cultural occasion, encompassing dancing, singing, and dramatics. It is worth mentioning that different theatrical forms practiced in Himachal Pradesh include Karyala, Bhagat, Banthara, Haran, Barlaj, etc.

Folk theatre is a powerful tool of communication and dissemination in rural areas, conveying the right message to the local people. However, with the passage of time, the dimension of folk theatre has changed and it is gradually becoming obsolete. It is pertinent to mention here that folk theatre is a very old cultural activity that signifies the rituals, heritage, and customs of the areas, based on legends, folklore, the past, beliefs, culture, traditions, conduct, etc. Undeniably, the 21st century has witnessed new technological means of communication through electronic devices. However, nobody can underestimate the hidden potential of folk theatre. This ancient form of communication remains an acknowledged tool in rural areas, where it continues to touch the constant sentiments and emotions of rural people.

Folk theatre is an enchanting and dynamic folk art that reflects the cultural heritage and traditions of a society. It has a rich history and serves as a means of communication, entertainment, and cultural expression. By combining elements of music, dance, storytelling, and drama, folk theatre creates a captivating experience that resonates with audiences.

Folk theatre holds a special significance as it allows communities to collectively tell stories and preserve their cultural narratives. It serves as a repository of history, mythology, and folk tales, passing them down from one generation to the next. Through colourful costumes, rhythmic music, and expressive movements, folk theatre brings these stories and characters to life, creating a profound connection with the audience.

One of the important characteristics of folk theatre is its accessibility and comprehensiveness. Unlike formal theatre, which often requires specialized training and resources, folk theatre emerges from the grassroots, involving the participation of ordinary people within the community. Folk theatre blurs the lines between performers and spectators, encouraging active involvement and fostering a sense of shared ownership.

Folk theatre serves multiple purposes beyond mere entertainment. It acts as a catalyst for social cohesion, fostering a sense of belonging and unity among society members. It addresses social issues, satirizes societal norms, and provides a platform for cultural critique.

One of the forms of folk theatre in Himachal Pradesh is Karyala. Karyala is one of the oldest forms of folk theatre, which is quite famous in some areas of Himachal Pradesh. It is a flexible theatre performed by artists without any script or directions. *Karyala* is an impromptu theatre that exists solely in the collective consciousness of the local community.

The Karyala presents itself in a vibrant array of colours, embodied in the dance, acting, singing, and humour displayed by the local people and rural inhabitants who participate in the hill folklore. Through their performance, they express a range of emotions, including happiness, joy, sorrow, distress, love, and concern for their community. While being a form of entertainment, this performance also serves as a means of artistic expression. It does not adhere to a specific time frame and can be showcased at any given moment, allowing for spontaneous and dynamic presentations.

The use of statements, dialogues, and couplets, along with the beating of *dhols*, *drums*, *Nagaras*, and other traditional instruments, is employed to celebrate and entertain gatherings. The practice of *Karyala* is common, similar to other folk theatre forms in the country. This mode of communication is a significant tool to sensitize and entertain rural people.

Thus, gathering for social events and communicating through gestures, dialogues, couplets, and other means is at the heart of social ordering. This theatre conveys messages, ideas, and opinions to the local community, nurturing their minds with information, knowledge, and facts, and compelling their intellectual growth and reasoning about the surrounding events. It is also a strong method of preserving heritage and culture in a feasible and integrated form. Folk theatre forms are a powerful medium of communication.

Karyala, as one of the famous folk theatres, is an affordable form of entertainment and a good medium for communicating information to the local people. It imparts social wisdom at an accessible level. Through these performances, artists act continuously with concentration and employ appropriate expressions to convey information among the rural community. Nowadays, with the widespread availability of internet facilities, numerous short stories, plays, and theatre performances are also accessible, conveying messages to the larger community. Even the telecast of Ramayana and Mahabharata during the Covid-19 pandemic aimed to inspire and entertain viewers while instilling important religious messages. However, the epic stories from these sources are already known to us and are continuously demonstrated through films, dramas, serials, plays, etc., to strengthen our religious and ethical values. In contrast, folk theatres concentrate on various momentary local emerging issues and highlight the kind of menace that is not good for the community at large.

Folk Media as the Voice of Folk Communities

Folk media stands apart as a distinct mode of communication, serving as a conduit for transmitting cultural traditions from one generation to the next. It consists of various forms such as folk music, songs, dances, and folk theatre, etc. Folk media encapsulates the essence of specific cultures and offers a window into traditional entertainment.

One of the significant characteristics of folk media is its inherent flexibility and adaptability to adjust to the needs and demands of a changing society. It seamlessly reflects the traditions and customs of communities, revealing the inner beauty and standards that exist deep within society. By preserving and promoting folk media, we not only safeguard our heritage but also foster a deeper understanding and appreciation for the richness of our diverse societies. In this way, folk media acts as a cultural bridge, connecting the past and present of a society.

In folk media, the term "folks" refers to people who belong to the same culture, language, and religion, while "media" represents the medium used for communication. According to Dudes (1965), the term "folk" can refer to any group of people who share at least one common factor. It does not matter what the linking factor is; it could be a common occupation, language, or religion. What is important is that a group formed for whatever reason will have some traditions which it calls its own (p.2). Thus, "folks" means people who belong to the same culture or share at least one common factor that associates them with each other. This factor could be a shared occupation, language, religion, geographic location, or any other characteristic that brings individuals together. When a group forms, it naturally develops its own set of traditions and customs unique to their collective identity.

Traditions within a folk group emerge as a result of shared experiences, values, and beliefs. These traditions serve as a means of expressing and preserving their collective identity, history, and cultural heritage. They can manifest in various forms, including folk music, dance, art, storytelling, cuisine, rituals, and festivals.

It's important to note that folk traditions are not confined to any specific cultural or geographical context. They can be found in diverse communities worldwide, each with its own unique set of customs and practices. Folk traditions are dynamic and evolve over time, adapting to changing circumstances while still retaining core elements that define the group's cultural identity.

Every folk group has its own folklore. The term 'folklore' was coined in 1846 by an Englishman, William John Thomas, replacing the earlier awkward term "popular antiquities" that had been derived from the root German word "Volklehre," which means the customs of the people (Punia, 1993, p.11). Folklore is learned informally and is part of daily life experience and unofficial knowledge about the world, communities, beliefs, cultures, and traditions that is expressed creatively through words, music, customs, actions, behaviours, and materials.

Folklore is that branch of culture which describes people's socio-cultural systems, beliefs, values, and attitudes through folk arts. It promotes the customs and traditions of the people and the process of socialization. Folklore is that field of culture which communicates the rich treasure of human experiences with the folks. Folk art portrays the picture of social life and the beauty hidden in daily life and the culture. It is the united aspiration and appearance of village life or rural areas. It is extremely connected with customs, traditions, and beliefs.

India has a rich cultural heritage, and being one of the ancient civilizations in the world, it is full of folklores, mythical stories, and legends of great men and women. Literature is the mirror of society, and Indian literature is no exception. Whether written or oral, the impact of both is the same. But in many places, oral literature plays a vital role in projecting the socio-cultural lives of society. Many of our cultural legacies, customs, social values, and rituals are passed on through generations through verbal communication. Similarly, traditional folk media is imparted and nurtured through oral sources, without following any specific grammar.

Traditional media is a more accepted medium of communication in rural areas. Folk media is mainly concerned with appealing to emotions. Traditional folk media is a powerful medium of expression for the people and their feelings. Folk media is not only a tool of communication but is also connected with the culture and ethnic identity of the people. Folk media serves various functions like communication, information, education, and entertainment, besides developing emotional bonding among them.

Folk media has a wider field consisting of various kinds of folk art, folk music, folklore, and folk drama. Traditional media are local forms of communication that have their roots in the particular culture of the community.

Folk media is of a unique nature and is nurtured through oral sources, without any grammar or literature. It provides channels of communication for expressing the social, ritual, ethical, and emotional needs of the people belonging to the community. Traditional folk media is different from new media as it caters to the attention of the ethno-rural audience. It connects better with rural people as they can relate to the things happening in the performances, as their roots are the same. They can easily connect with it emotionally, as it reflects their society like a mirror and provides a better understanding of the things happening around them. It also offers a better understanding of society, culture, and rituals.

Historical Background:

In India, every state has its own folk art forms. When discussing the origin of folk forms, it can be said that they originated from primitive Indian traditions and were passed down from one generation to another. Historians have recorded that during the First World War (1919), Dipchand, one of the famous composers of 'Swaang' (the popular rural drama of East Punjab), formed a folk drama troupe and successfully persuaded several young lads from Haryana to join the defence forces. For his productive use of folk theatre, he was rewarded by the then British Government (Parmar, 1975, p.18). This indicates that before independence, folk media played an important role in disseminating messages and motivating people.

Rani (1996) points out that in the 1950s, folk performing arts were employed to create awareness about the Five Year Plans. As early as 1952, the first Five Year Plan had recommended the utilization of folk media for all developmental activities (p.2). The Song and Drama Division of the Union Ministry of Information and Broadcasting was created by the Government of India in 1954. Its purpose was to use live entertainment to educate and inform people in rural areas.

The first remarkable global recognition of communication through folk media in developing countries came in 1972 when UNESCO organized a series of meetings in London regarding the use of folk media for Family Planning communication programs. In the digital age of new media, where information flows rapidly, folk media retains its unique essence of communication, providing healthy entertainment to the masses, particularly in rural areas of the country.

Significance of Folk Media in Cultural Communication

The importance of traditional media has also been cited in the MacBride Commission's report "Many Voices, One World" (1982) by the International Commission for the Study of Communication Problems. The report states, "Extensive experience shows that traditional forms of communication can be effective in dispelling superstitions, archaic perceptions, and unscientific attitudes that people inherit as part of tradition, and which are difficult to modify if the benefits of change are hard to demonstrate" (p.81). Furthermore, the report states, "Practitioners of traditional media use a subtle form of persuasion by presenting the required message in locally popular artistic forms. This cannot be rivaled by any other means of communication"(p.81).

This report emphasizes how traditional forms of communication can effectively address and dispel superstitions, outdated beliefs, and unscientific attitudes that are deeply rooted in cultural traditions. It suggests that changing these ingrained beliefs can be difficult unless the advantages of change are clearly demonstrated. In simpler terms, the report shows how traditional communication methods can help people let go of old, irrational beliefs by showing them the benefits of embracing new and more rational perspectives.

Traditional media practitioners employ a subtle form of persuasion by presenting messages through locally popular artistic forms. These traditional forms of communication have an inherent advantage in connecting with people on an emotional and cultural level. The use of artistic expressions helps bridge the gap between the new information being conveyed and the existing beliefs or perceptions deeply embedded within the cultural fabric.

The report suggests that traditional forms of communication are powerful tools for social change because they offer an effective strategy to challenge and transform outdated mindsets. By presenting messages within familiar cultural contexts, these communication methods can gradually shift attitudes, dispel superstitions, and promote scientific thinking. The inherent trust and acceptance associated with traditional media can aid in overcoming resistance to change and facilitate a more receptive environment for new ideas and knowledge.

India, a land of abundant cultural and folk heritage, thrives on the essence of its traditional forms of communication. These age-old folk media channels play a vital role in upholding social norms, imparting religious knowledge, and nurturing wisdom, ultimately keeping the social structure harmoniously intact. One of the most remarkable aspects of traditional folk media is its ability to generate a shared conscience. Within the realm of folk arts, a magical transformation takes place, blurring the lines between actors and audience. Both the artists and the spectators seamlessly merge into a cohesive whole, becoming an inseparable part of the vibrant social fabric.

Role of Folk Theatre in Cultural Transformation

In India, folk theatre plays a significant role in cultural transformation. It is a popular form of entertainment among the common people and is closely connected to their feelings and expressions. Folk theatre combines various elements such as dance, music, and poetry, creating a rich artistic experience. According to Varadpande (1979), theatre encompasses a wide range of human activities, portraying the complexity of human life. *Natya*, as defined by Bharata, represents the diverse human characters through appropriate abhinaya (expression). Therefore, the theatre reflects and portrays human life and activities in an engaging manner that entertains the audience.

Benegal (1968) explains that dramatic representation can be classified into three forms: *Natya*, which involves gestures and language (drama); *Nritya*, which relies on gestures without language (pantomime); and *Nritta*, which focuses on pure dancing. Drama can be further divided into two categories: *Lokadharmi* or realistic, which depicts ordinary people in ordinary situations without embellishment, and *Natyadharmi* or conventional, which is more theatrical in nature. It is important to note that these distinctions should be understood carefully.

One example of folk theatre is Karyala, which is famous in Himachal Pradesh and associated with the districts of Solan, Shimla, and Sirmour. Karyala is considered a lokadharmi drama as it entertains and simultaneously raises awareness among the public about social evils and their societal impact. Through various swangs (acts), Karyala artists effectively convey important messages to the audience, fostering cultural transformation and contributing to social development.

Folk theatre in Indian villages encompasses the entirety of the inner personalities of its inhabitants, striving to fulfil their intellectual, artistic, and emotional needs. It incorporates a wide range of expressions including dance, music, and dialogue. This diverse approach culminates in a form of self-contained and captivating entertainment for the audience. It provides a complete emotional experience and fosters an environment conducive to effortless communication.

Folk theatre in Indian villages fulfills the intellectual, artistic, and emotional needs of the local community, providing comprehensive entertainment. It incorporates various artistic elements, including dance, music, and dialogue, creating a rich and immersive experience for the audience. Through folk theatre, the audience embarks on a complete emotional journey, experiencing a range of emotions such as joy, sadness, excitement, and empathy. Additionally, folk theatre fosters a sense of community and unity among the audience. The shared experience of watching the performances creates a collective bond and a sense of belonging. It serves as a platform for social interaction, enabling people to come together, celebrate, and connect with their cultural heritage.

Folk theatre in Indian villages offers a comprehensive and captivating form of entertainment that addresses the intellectual, artistic, and emotional requirements of the local community. It integrates diverse artistic elements to create an immersive and self-contained experience for the audience. Folk theatre serves as a seamless mode of communication, promoting a sense of unity and safeguarding cultural traditions within the community.

Karyala folk theatre freely employs dialogues and dance as its main elements to entertain the rural masses. Its primary objective is to depict the essence of village life and fulfill the emotional and artistic needs of the rural people. Karyala creates an engaging and delightful environment for communication. Communication mediums that are unfamiliar and distant from the local culture tend to have less impact and significance. Therefore, Karyala, being relatable and accessible to the rural masses, holds great importance and resonates with them.

Therefore, Karyala folk theatre, being familiar and closely connected to the rural masses, is sociable and resonates strongly with them. According to Mathur (1964) "In Indian villages have been much more than a spontaneous expression of folk-life or a local folk- device to entertain the community. It is both on off-shoot of and a root that has nourished the traditional, classical culture of India"(p.4). The folk theatre in Indian villages is more than just a natural form of entertainment or a way to express local traditions. It has played a significant role in both influencing and preserving the traditional and classical culture of India. In simpler terms, folk theatre is like a branch that has grown out of, and at the same time, nourished the rich cultural heritage of the country.

REFERENCES

Aggarwal, Vir Bala and Gupta,V.S.(2001). *Handbook of Journalism and Mass Communication.* New Delhi: Concept Publishing Company.

Bandura, Albert (1977). *Social learning Theory.* Standford University: Prentice-Hall.

Benegal, Som (1968).*A panorama of theatre in India.* Bombay: Indian Council for Cultural Relation Popular Prakashan.

Dundes, Alan (1965).*The Study of folklore.* USA: Prentice-Hall.

Dundes, Alan (1980).Interpreting folklore. Bloomington: Indiana University Press.

Gargi, Balwant (1991).*Folk Theatre of India.* Noida: Rupa.Co.

Mishra. Raghavendra (Eds.).*Traditional folk Media in India Practice& Relevance* (pp.181-189). Varanasi: Bharti Prakashan.

MacBride, Sean (1980).*Many voices One world.* Paris: United Nations Educational, Scientific and Cultural Organisation.

Mathur, J.C.(1964).*Drama in Rural India.* Bombay: Asia Publishing House

Parmar, Shyam (1975 2nded). *Traditional Folk Media in India.* New Delhi: Geka Books.

Punia, Deep (1993). Social values in Folklore. Jaipur and New Delhi: Rawat Publication

Rani, N. Usha (1996). *Folk Media for Development.* Mysore: Karnataka Book Publishers.

Varadpande, M.L.(1979).*Traditions of Indian Theatre.* New Delhi: Abhinav Publication.

Varadpande, M.L.(1989).Invitation to Indian Theatre. New Delhi: Arnold Publisher.

JOURNALS

Bhardwaj, Harsh (2016).Folk Theatre in India: Role, needs and challenges.*Worldreader*,1,1-6. https://docplayer.net/60676945-Folk-theatre-in-india-role-needs-and-challenges.html

Edinyangand David, Sunday (2016). The significance of social learning theories in the Teaching of social studies education. *International Journal of Sociology and Anthropology Research,*2,40-45.https://www.eajournals.org/wp-content/uploads/The-Significance-of-Social-Learning-Theories-in-the-Teaching-of-Social-Studies-Education.pdf

Kumar, Deepak (2015).Folk Theatre in India: Role, Needs and Challenges.*World Wide Journal of Multidisciplinary Research and Development*,2(9),49-51. http://wwjmrd.com/upload/folk-theatre-in-india-role-needs-and-challenges_1553261009.pdf

Kodavath, Yathish L.(2015).Traditional Media for rural development and effective communication.*Indian Journal of Applied Research*,5,19-21.

Malhan,P.N.(1986).National media Policy.*Vidura*,1,1.

Shaika, Shahi, Lal, Ruhi,Jonjua, Mehak (2021).Sustainable Development Goal: Case Study of using folk media as a potent tool in India.*Journal of Contemporary Issues in Business and Government*,27,4426-4443. https://cibg.org.au/pdf_10530_3a08ded1a3e23b20fdd3a552e00defd9.html

Chapter -2

Karyala

Himachal Pradesh, known as Dev Bhumi, is situated in the heart of the Western Himalayas. Physiographically, the territory can be divided into three zones: the outer Himalayas or the Shiwaliks, the inner Himalayas or mid-mountain region, and the greater Himalayas or alpine zone. The majority of the people in Himachal Pradesh follow the Hindu faith and are devoted to traditional gods. They hold strong beliefs in village deities, who are considered gods, heroes, or Rishi's and serve as a source of inspiration for the villagers. These deities are commonly referred to as *Devta.*

Every village in Himachal Pradesh has a temple where people assemble for worship. The belief is that local deities hold responsibility for bringing timely rain, ensuring good harvests, and granting other favors. People also believe that if these deities are not worshiped properly, they become angry and, in their anger, allow evil spirits to prey on the village and its inhabitants in the form of diseases and other calamities. The people in the hill areas also hold belief in the existence of evil spirits that disturb their peace. Consequently, people worship local deities to protect themselves from these malevolent powers. The common belief is that by worshiping the local gods, the villagers are guarded against the adverse effects of these spirits.

The people of Himachal Pradesh possess a very rich cultural heritage, as evidenced by the wide variety of folk dances and folk dramas. It is worth mentioning that folk theatre is a composite art form in India, incorporating elements from music, dance, performance, epics, religious practices, and ethical dissemination. Its roots lie in native culture, deeply embedded in the local identity and social values of a particular society or region. These folk theatres are prevalent in Rajasthan, Haryana, Uttar Pradesh, Punjab, Madhya Pradesh, and other areas. Himachal Pradesh is no exception, as folk theatre remains a common practice alongside modern developments. The purpose of folk theatre extends beyond entertainment; it also serves to disseminate the values necessary for strengthening societal values.

In the words of Bascom, the concept of folk theatre embodies two ideas as cited by Ahluwalia(1995)

(i) that it was evolved over great stretches of time by communal practice; and

(ii) that the process of handing on through successive generations operates within a framework of natural selection and an unconscious choice of the more acceptable spectacles.

These ideas highlight the natural and communal nature of folk theatre. It is a living tradition that has developed and evolved over time through the collective participation and practice of a community. The successful spectacles and performances that resonate with audiences are passes over from one generation to the next, ensuring the survival of the folk theatre tradition..

Folk dramas play a significant role as a form of entertainment in Himachal Pradesh. They are characterized as impromptu theatre and are typically performed during the winter season, following the busy months of sowing and harvesting. The villagers gather in a temple or village square and enjoy folk dramas throughout the night. Karyala folk theatre stands as one of the oldest forms of folk theatre in Himachal Pradesh.

Karyala folk theatre distinguishes itself from modern theatre in several ways. Firstly, it is performed without a predefined story, script, or director. Surprisingly, Karyala theatre is executed by the actors without any prior rehearsal or script. This traditional form of theatre is prevalent in the majority parts of Shimla, Solan, and Sirmour districts of Himachal Pradesh. The artists involved in Karyala are considered natural-born artists, as they do not undergo any formal training specifically for performance purposes.

Everything happens instantly within the minds of the artists, and they perform informally without the need for a stage. Karyala is a folk theatre that is played without a script, producer, director, props, and rehearsal. It is an open-air theatre and does not require a specific stage setup. The performances take place in open grounds or *Khalyans*. The majority of the performances are held around Diwali. Thakur (2006) pointed out that Late S.S.S Thakur who was himself a great actor, director and producer of dramas and once Chief Producer of A.I.R. made notable inserts into the growth and evolution of *Karyala*. Under project of Sangeet Natak Akademi he staged two separate *Karyala* plays- one based on traditional theme and oral dialogue and the other on written script. Subsequently, the Akademi published his booklet '*Karyala*, Folk Theatre of Himachal Pradesh' in 1985"(p.168).

According to Thakur, there are differences regarding the etymological origin of the word "karyala." Some relate it to the "Kreednniykam" of Bharatmuni, while others associate it with the local fragrant flower known as Karyal, specifically the Kachnaar, a famous blossom. There is another Pahari word, "Karel," which means to unearth some secret. It might have a reference to the word "karail," which means a vow or request to the deity for the fulfilment of a certain wish.

Some scholars are of the opinion that *Karyala* originated from the word '*Karal*' which means to dig or to explore. *Karyala* also means *Kachnar*; *kural* is the name of a bird. *Karyala* or *Karala* also means to overturn, upturn or to make someone conscious. There are others who believe that it is related to the word '*Karal*' which means 'to pledge'. People thank the deity on the fulfilment of their pledge in the temple (Ahluwalia, 1995, p.30). So, while the word '*Karyala*' has different meanings, it is clear from the above information that it is organized with the purpose of fulfilling a wish and is devoted to the local deity.

Origin and Development

Truly speaking, based on the available information from existing literature, it is evident that nobody really knows about the origin of Karyala as a folk theatre in the state of Himachal Pradesh. Some distorted glimpses of information received from artists, performers, audiences, and a few scholars suggest that this traditional practice was performed (and seems to have originated) during the Vaishnav Bhakti movement of the 15th or 16th century. Some theorists and artists believe that *Karyala*, as a traditional folk form, must be very ancient, while others consider its inclusion in the classification of Bharatmuni's Natyashastra.

According to Shri Masaddi Ram, one of the performers of Karyala folk theatre, referenced by Ashok Hans in his research, Karyala is an ancient theatrical form that originated during the time of King Junag, a former princely state. King Junag was a revered ruler and deity in his region. However, Dev Shirgul, a local deity belonging to a few clustered villages of Sirmour and Shimla, dethroned nearby the entire Junag State. He was a despotic monarch always in the habit of creating troubles. One of the communities loyal to King Junag, called Pariharh, engaged in conflict with Shirgul but couldn't defeat him. To seek assistance, Pariharh was sent to Kashmir to ask for help from King Bijeshwar of Bijwara. King Bijeshwar arrived to fight against Shirgul, and when Shirgul rained iron-hails on the enemies. King Bijeshwar used his natural powers to create lightning and thunderbolts, forcing Shirgul to flee. Thus, from the above narrated story, it is believed that these kings were bestowed with godly powers. It is pertinent to mention here that Bijeshwar is known as Deo 'Biju' in the local dialect and villagers organize Karyala in honour of Deo Biju and for the fulfilment of their wishes.

Bijeshawar (Bijju) Devta Temple (Solan)

Although the above information does not clarify the origin of Karyala, it does state that Karyala is devoted to a particular local deity.

Artistry of Karyala Folk Theatre Performers

There is no formal training provided to the *Karyala* artists; instead, they are self-educated. They observe the behaviour of village functionaries and entertain others through parody and satire. The language used by the performers is loutish, inelegant, and ungrammatical, but it resonates with the rural folks, who enjoy it. *Karyala* humour is predominantly verbal, which is why people are interested in the dramatic words used by *Karyala* artists. The beauty of *Karyala* lies in the absurdity of sharp comments on people and events, conveyed through the misuse of words, fractured grammar.

The *Karyala* party assembles in November after the harvest. It is a multi-ethnic and secular gathering, with villagers from all castes participating in a cooperative manner. The selection of artists is based on natural talent for mimicry, jest, and ecstasy.

A 'Scene' in Karyala

The wonderful thing about Karyala is that such amusement is endowed with minimal expenses. Even in today's time of vastly commercialized shows, the *Karyalchis* can be invited for a meagre amount. All that is given to them is a small sum of rupees and food on the night of performances.

Institution of Vidushak or Sutradhar

In the Indian folk theatre, the *Sutradhar* holds the most significant role in the entire folk drama, known by different names in the various regional diversities. In a way, he plays an important part in the evolution of folk theatre itself. The narrators of the folk theatre make art and its impact more visual. Their narrations make it simpler to understand the story underlying different roles. The *Sutradhar* is an excellent means of translating any story into a logical dramatic production. They are the ones who narrate or relate the story while also assisting the actors. They effortlessly create the background, leaving the arena for the artists to interpret their messages through theatrical action. According to Gargi (1991) "he has the freedom to connect the past with the present and relate the drama to contemporary scene. He also acts as a liaison between the audience and the player."(p.5).

The folk entertainer found the direct intervention of the narrator to carry out many important dramatic functions more convenient because here he establishes a rapport with the audience across the stage and explain things in a much more intimate manner. Thus, it is crystal clear from the above that the role of the *Sutradhar* in Karyala is integral. They are the key person to maintain the linkage between artists and spectators. To disseminate the true messages through Karyala folk theatre, they initially narrate or create an amicable environment with the audience to convey the direct message through the performance in rural areas. This kind of communication through Karyala serves as a tool to sensitize the people while providing entertainment.

Folk theatres, on the whole, are narrative in character, with social, religious, or moral communication and messages to be conveyed. The *Sutradhar* plays a crucial role in maintaining the quality of narration in folk plays. They manage the play and introduce breaks in the continuity of the performance. The presence of the *Sutradhar* became important due to the peculiar characteristics of folk plays, where there is hardly any written or well-defined script. They provide clues to the artists, allowing them to improvise their dialogues on the spur of the moment.

In the practice of Karyala, the *Sutradhar* plays a crucial role in capturing momentary attention. They instantly give clues that are then responded to by the actors, conveying instant and relevant social messages to the audience. The *Sutradhar* remains present on the stage throughout the performance to guide its course into a coherent theatrical pattern. They conduct the proceedings according to the traditions of the particular folk drama. Moreover, they provide general information about the play, including its story and the name of the author. They also define the time and place of the action.

Generally, the Sutradhar introduces the characters of the play to the audience by announcing their entry, taking them to it, or asking questions that lead to the revelation of their identity. Their role also involves describing scenes or events of the play that cannot be shown on the stage, as well as off-stage happenings. They weave different story patterns that are then performed by the actors accordingly. The Sutradhar maintains the logical significance of the actors' performances and draws the attention and confidence of the audience. In essence, they serve as the announcer or narrator of the play and also impersonate a character themselves to capture everyone's attention.

Make-up of Karyala Artists

The makeup of Karyala artists is indigenous and low-priced. The performers, usually belonging to local areas and different families, consist of 11-12 artists, though the number can be increased if needed. Some of them specialize in playing conventional musical instruments, while others take on multiple roles, including singing and dancing. Anyone who possesses the knowledge of playing instruments can join the Karyala party.

The makeup materials used by *Karyalchee*'s are simple and locally sourced. They use white wheat flour for a white color effect, black from the *tava* or skillet (the chapatti cooking iron plate), and red from *geroo*, a local red-colored earth. Wigs and beards are made using jute and other easily accessible fibres. Masks are prepared from tree barks, pulp, as well as carved wood.

Performance with inexpensive make-up

This shows that the practice of Karyala is performed locally and remains famous in the majority of the districts. Another prominent feature highlighted is that the artists use local fibres, clothes, and traditional colors to perform this activity, making the makeup of folk theatre artists appear inexpensive.

Use of jute and fibre for beard

Artist performing Karyala

References

Ahluwalia,Kailash.(1995). *Karyala:An Impromptu Theatre of Himachal Pradesh.*New Delhi:Reliance Publishing House.

Gargi, Balwant.(1991).*Folk Theatre of India*. Noida: Rupa.Co.

Hans, Ashok.(1986). *Karyala A folk theatrical form of Himachal Pradesh.*Delhi:Sahitya Sahakar.

Mathur, J.C.(1964).*Drama in Rural India*. Bombay: Asia Publishing House.

Parmar,Shayam.(1975).*Traditional folk media in India.*New Delhi:Geka books.

Thakur, M.R.(2006).*Folklore of Himachal Pradesh*. New Delhi: Indus Publishing Company.

Thakur, S.S.S. *Karyala folk theatre of Himachal Pradesh*. New Delhi:Sangeet Natak Akademi.

सन्दर्भ ग्रन्थ सूची :

पुस्तक

हाण्डा, ओमचन्द. (1988). पश्चिमी हिमालय की लोक कलाएं. नई दिल्ली : इण्डस

पब्लिशिंग कम्पनी.

बंसल, परमानन्द. (2005). हिमाचली लोकनाट्य धाज्जा सांस्कृतिक तथा संगीतिक अध्ययन.

दिल्ली : संजय प्रकाशन.

व्यथित, गौतम. शर्मा. (2007). हिमाचली ग्रामीण रंगमंच यात्रा. दिल्ली : राजभाषा प्रकाशन.

गौतम, खुशीराम. (1992). हिमाचल प्रदेश का लोक साहित्य सिरमौरी लोक साहित्य. शिमला : हिमाचल कला, संस्कृति एवं भाषा अकादमी.

ठाकुर, एम. आर. (1981). हिमाचल के लोकनाट्य और लोकानुरंजन. दिल्ली : हिमाचल पुस्तक भण्डार.

पत्रिकाएँ

आहलूवालिया, कैलाश. (1989). करियाला : कुछ प्रश्न. सोमसी, 61-65

शास्त्री, शशिकांत. (1983). हिमाचल लोकनाट्य स्वरूप एवं परम्परा. सोमसी, 32-35

आहलूवालिया, कैलाश. (1977). लोकनाट्य-परम्परा और सम्भावना. सोमसी, 27-30

ठाकुर, एम. आर. (1988). करियाला. सोमसी, 85-89

हाण्डा, ओमचन्द. (1975). हिमाचल का लोकनाट्य : करियाला. सोमसी, 25-29

शर्मा, एच. आनन्द. (2019). करियालची. सोमसी, 45-48

देव, अमर. (2017). लोकनाट्य की जीवंत मिसाल करियाला, बरलाज व धाज्जा. हिमप्रस्थ, 151-154

अरुण, नरेंद्र. (2008). हिमाचली लोकनाट्य विधाएं. हिमप्रस्थ, 18-23

अजनबी, नेमचन्द. (2005). लोकनाट्य व लोकानुरंजन. हिमप्रस्थ, 8-14

हंस, अशोक. (2005). करियाला. हिमप्रस्थ, 66-70

हंस, अशोक. (2004). करियाला : एक लोकरंगमंचीय रूप. हिमप्रस्थ, 13-15

ठाकुर, गौरी. शंकर. (1999). हिमाचली लोकनाट्य परम्परा में करियाला. हिमप्रस्थ, 3-7

ललित, सी.आर.बी. (1994). हिमाचल की लोकनाट्य परम्परा. हिमप्रस्थ, 5-7

Chapter -3

Acting Arena of Folk Theatre Karyala

The stage of Karyala is known as the 'akhara' (arena). It is set in a location that is visible from slopes and all around. In the middle of the arena, a huge fire is lit, which is considered sacred and holy. Earthen pots or torch lights called mashal's are tied to the poles around the akhara. A green room is arranged on one side for the purpose of preparation.

In simple terms, the *Akhara* serves as the sanctum sanctorum for performing Karyala. It is illuminated by *Mashal*'s to captivate the attention of all the people, who act as the audience. Local arrangements are made, such as a dilapidated hut covered by curtains, to serve as a changing room.

Karyala performers, known as *karyalchis*, typically choose an open ground (*khalyan*) for their performances. The performance area within the karyala is called *khada* (*akhara*). Inside the *khada*, a bonfire known as *ghiana* is lit, which is considered highly sacred and kept burning throughout the play. The bonfire serves multiple purposes, including providing warmth to the artists, protecting them from the cold, warding off evil spirits, and serving as a source of lighting.

Artists with Bonfire called *Ghiana*

Artists in the arena

As per religious beliefs, the fire in Karyala is considered sacred and provides protection against evil powers. The burning fire symbolizes the true spirit of the performance, as it is always present, signifying the presence of protective spiritual spirits. Another significant feature worth highlighting is that the presence of fire provides heat to the people and actors. This is especially important because, as mentioned earlier, Karyala is performed in open spaces, mostly during winters.

Musical Instruments

The performance of Karyala is unique and distinctive in the hilly areas of Himachal Pradesh. It is liked by rural people and is not solely performed by actors in isolation. To make the event more engaging and effective in communication, traditional musical instruments are also incorporated. These instruments hold their own religious significance and are used in a specific sequence based on the theme, story, and play being performed. One notable feature of Karyala performances is the starting point. At the very beginning, instruments like *Nagaara* are played loudly, allowing their rhythm to reach a long distance. This serves as a symbol for the commencement of the Karyala folk theatre. For this traditional musical artistic performance, instruments such as *Harmonium*, *Nafeeri*, *Ransinga*, *Nagaara*, *Shehnai*, and *Dhol* are used.

Charm of Local Language Humour in Folk Drama Dialogues

Words are the instruments used to convey meaning. India is a country with a multitude of dialects and languages, with language changing every few kilo meters. Similarly, in Himachal Pradesh, the language varies based on geographical differences. The dialogues and language used in Karyala are rooted in the local nature. Villagers can better understand and relate to things when conveyed in their local language. This is one of the reasons why Karyala is highly popular in these three districts.

Karyala is an impromptu theatre that relies entirely on the wit and sense of humor of the artists. Its main features include being performed without a written script and living within the minds of the performers. These theatres do not require an educated audience or qualified scriptwriters. They simply need the art of humour in the natural village environment, focusing on rustic characters and themes.

Thus, wit becomes a powerful tool for entertainment in Karyala. Wit encompasses intellectual quickness, raillery, and repartee performed by the artists. It is closely related to humour and acts as a sharp weapon that can cut through both the good and the bad. It is predominantly present among non-literate folks rather than urban audiences.

A Powerful Medium of Expression

Karyala is a folk theatre of the common man, providing them with the liberty to criticize cruelty and discrimination perpetrated by the authorities. In olden times, it served as the best means of communication when no other avenues were available. It was also a powerful medium for expressing complaints to the authorities. Thus, Karyala served a purpose beyond entertainment. Through these performances, authorities would receive cues about their mistakes, making it a natural way to convey concerns in front of them. Karyala is an exceptional form of drama where people can purge their feelings and emotions that they may otherwise be unable to express.

In simple words, without direct interaction with the administration, *Karyalchis* convey their messages informally through Karyala. Thus, Karyala folk theatre can be seen as a tool of communication to inform the administration about grievances. This mechanism is straightforward, and the presence of mind of the *Karyalchis* plays a significant role.

Humour possesses the ability to modify messages in numerous ways. Firstly, it can add a light-hearted and playful tone to communication, making it more engaging, relatable, and enjoyable for the audience. By injecting humour into messages, the delivery becomes more entertaining and captivating, capturing the attention and interest of the recipients.

Moreover, humour can be employed to convey complex or sensitive information in a more digestible and accessible manner. It serves as a bridge between challenging or abstract concepts and the audience's understanding, helping to simplify and clarify messages that may otherwise be difficult to grasp. Through the use of humour, communication becomes more approachable and memorable, increasing the likelihood of the message being retained and understood.

Therefore, humour is an integral aspect of communication that can modify messages across all mediums and instruments of expression. It adds entertainment value, simplifies complex information, enhances connection, and holds persuasive potential. By harnessing the power of humour, communicators can engage, captivate, and effectively convey their messages to a wide range of audiences.

A 'Scene' in Karyala

Karyala not only entertains the audience but also serves as a *lok dharma natak*, addressing problems and grievances to the authorities. Through Karyala swang acts, unwritten petitions are presented in front of the authorities, demanding their attention. This form of theatre provides a platform for expressing unfulfilled desires. The aims of various swangs include both entertainment and instruction, and they are closely related to daily life and social issues.

Awareness through entertainment

The swangs play a vital role in communication within Karyala. Through these swangs, various segments of society and significant issues are addressed using day-to-day examples. Importantly, these swangs shed light on the weaknesses and flaws within the existing societal structure. Disparities in living standards, cultural practices, administrative workings, and the need for significant improvements are depicted in a pleasant and interesting systematic manner. It is noteworthy that the entire Karyala folk theatre serves as entertainment, allowing the villagers to enjoy the dual purpose of this activity. The *Karyalchees*, through their roles, provide a great deal of amusement while sensitizing the masses to crucial issues.

Variety of entertainment

Frankly speaking, at the grassroots level, these artists in Karyala serve as the real social reformers, aiming to eradicate the prevalent evil practices in rural areas. Additionally, an outstanding feature of Karyala is the integration of songs, dance, acting, and performance as inherent parts of the art form. The Chandravali dance, folk songs, traditional local artistic presentations, and the role of the Sutradhar (Vidushask) are considered the soul of Karyala.

This performance is generally conducted in the evening or before sunrise. The local people, having had their dinner, eagerly participate or observe as spectators in this Karyala folk theatre. It is worth mentioning that the Swangs in Karyala can be classified into various categories, including historical, ancient, social, and day-to-day activities, among others.

Production Journey of Karyala

To begin the Karyala performance, religious or sage-related couplets are recited. Following this, there will be announcements about mythological personalities, along with programs showcasing social and day-to-day activities in front of the villagers. Amidst these acts, the *Vidushak* appears unexpectedly, speaking illogically or logically and making comments that induce guffawing and giggling. Simultaneously, the performers engage in *Chandravali* dance accompanied by traditional local folk songs.

In reality, the role of the *Vidushak* holds immense importance in various forms of Karyala. The reason behind this is that the Vidushak's primary purpose is to entertain the local people, and in every explanation or performance, there are unique characters. Some may portray themselves as disciples of a sage, but their actions and performances are extraordinary, resulting in laughter and amusement among the local people and observers.

Lumberdar ka swang

Sahib ka swang

In the majority of performances, the Vidushak brings humor and makes comments on society at large. Through this approach, wrong practices and traditions in day-to-day life are highlighted, including those related to rishis, rich people, poor people, agriculturists, special castes, society natives, and workers. These various programs serve as examples within the Karyala folk theatre

Swangs in Karyala

The drama begins with the musicians playing the *badhai taal*, sitting on one side of the arena with their instruments. The music serves as a gathering call, capturing the attention of the audience from far and wide. Soon, *Chandrawali* enters the arena, becoming the main character and the centre of attraction in the play. *Chandrawali* is essentially a man adorned in women's clothing. She worships the *ghiana*, respectfully touches the musical instruments, and performs a ritual dance. She is followed by another artist known by different names, such as *sidha*, *topi wala*, *Dangra*, or *kanha*. Both artists dance together to the beats of *badhai taal*, followed by *Jang taal* and *Karyala taal*, before making a graceful exit.

Chandrawali* and *Topi wala

After the exit of both characters, two or three artists dressed in saffron costumes of *sadhus* (hermits) enter the *khada* with a loud voice saying, "*Alakh Niranjan*". Then, the real performance of the shows begins, traditionally known as Swangs or "mimicries," which involve amusing imitations where actors mimic the styles of others, often ridiculing them. The characters rely on wordplay to make the audience laugh. There are no written or recorded dialogues; everything is composed extemporaneously.

Significance of Swangs in Rural Communities

Swang is basically the mimicry (*Nakal*) of characters in the unique style of *Karyalchees*, inspired by their observations from everyday life. The performance relies on the artists' keen observation of the characters, their psychology, sociolinguistic and economic conflicts, as well as their habits, cultural practices, and present-day issues. It captures the essence of existing interests and portrays them through the art of mimicry.

Nat aur Nati ka Swang

The Swangs are presented in the form of dramatic music, freestyle singing without the aid of musical instruments, poetic couplets, dialogues, and the use of local idioms and proverbs. The performances incorporate mimicry, gestures, facial expressions, the use of eyes, and various sitting positions to enhance the storytelling. Many dialogues are well-remembered by the artists, while others are improvised on the spot. Some dialogues are also created and completed in the moment. Additionally, a few dialogues arise as responses and reactions from the audience. The audience members also actively participate by sharing their thoughts and comments about the Swangs and the Karyalchis, illustrating the involvement of the audience in the drama.

"Improvised dialogues of the characters are woven around those dialogues which are already in the Swangs, but with necessary arrangements as the situation demands during the performance, changing even the syntax of the words. When *Karyalchee's* sense that audience that audience is freely involved and intends more to witness and enjoy the Swang in that situation dialogues are framed immediately, depending on the natural genius of the performer".(Hans,1986,p.36). Therefore, Karyala artists are trained in a way that enables them to immediately manage songs, dialogues, and couplets. Since Karyala is a theatre performed without a script, it relies on oral communication and the ability to remember the content.

Sadhu ka Swang

There are many Swangs, and it is not necessary to present all of them in a sequential manner in a single performance. For example, "Sanyasi Ka Swang" is typically performed just after the completion of the Chandrawali Dance. The selection of Swangs for a particular night may depend on factors such as audience participation and the available time period. Additionally, new Swangs may emerge over time, adding to the repertoire of performances.

References

Ahluwalia,Kailash.(1995). *Karyala:An Impromptu Theatre of Himachal Pradesh.*New Delhi:Reliance Publishing House.

Gargi, Balwant.(1991).*Folk Theatre of India*. Noida: Rupa.Co.

Hans, Ashok.(1986). *Karyala A folk theatrical form of Himachal Pradesh.* Delhi:Sahitya Sahakar.

Mathur, J.C.(1964).*Drama in Rural India*. Bombay: Asia Publishing House.

Parmar,Shayam.(1975).*Traditional folk media in India.*New Delhi:Geka books.

Thakur, M.R.(2006).*Folklore of Himachal Pradesh*. New Delhi: Indus Publishing Company.

Thakur, S.S.S. *Karyala folk theatre of Himachal Pradesh*. New Delhi:Sangeet Natak Akademi.

सन्दर्भ ग्रन्थ सूची :

पुस्तक

हाण्डा, ओमचन्द. (1988). पश्चिमी हिमालय की लोक कलाएं. नई दिल्ली : इण्डस

पब्लिशिंग कम्पनी.

बंसल, परमानन्द. (2005). हिमाचली लोकनाट्य धाज्जा सांस्कृतिक तथा संगीतिक अध्ययन.

दिल्ली : संजय प्रकाशन.

व्यथित, गौतम. शर्मा. (2007). हिमाचली ग्रामीण रंगमंच यात्रा. दिल्ली : राजभाषा प्रकाशन.

गौतम, खुशीराम. (1992). हिमाचल प्रदेश का लोक साहित्य सिरमौरी लोक साहित्य. शिमला

: हिमाचल कला, संस्कृति एवं भाषा अकादमी.

ठाकुर, एम. आर. (1981). हिमाचल के लोकनाट्य और लोकानुरंजन. दिल्ली : हिमाचल

पुस्तक भण्डार.

पत्रिकाएँ

आहलूवालिया, कैलाश. (1989). करियाला : कुछ प्रश्न. सोमसी, 61-65

शास्त्री, शशिकांत. (1983). हिमाचल लोकनाट्य स्वरुप एवं परम्परा. सोमसी, 32-35

आहलूवालिया, कैलाश. (1977). लोकनाट्य-परम्परा और सम्भावना. सोमसी, 27-30

ठाकुर, एम. आर. (1988). करियाला. सोमसी, 85-89

हाण्डा, ओमचन्द. (1975). हिमाचल का लोकनाट्य : करियाला. सोमसी, 25-29

शर्मा, एच. आनन्द. (2019). करियालची. सोमसी, 45-48

देव, अमर. (2017). लोकनाट्य की जीवंत मिसाल करियाला, बरलाज व धाज्जा. हिमप्रस्थ,

151-154

अरुण, नरेंद्र. (2008). हिमाचली लोकनाट्य विधाएं. हिमप्रस्थ, 18-23

अजनबी, नेमचन्द. (2005). लोकनाट्य व लोकानुरंजन. हिमप्रस्थ, 8-14

हंस, अशोक. (2005). करियाला. हिमप्रस्थ, 66-70

हंस, अशोक. (2004). करियाला : एक लोकरंगमंचीय रुप. हिमप्रस्थ, 13-15

ठाकुर, गौरी. शंकर. (1999). हिमाचली लोकनाट्य परम्परा में करियाला. हिमप्रस्थ, 3-7

ललित, सी.आर.बी. (1994). हिमाचल की लोकनाट्य परम्परा. हिमप्रस्थ, 5-7

Chapter -4

Social Awareness Through Various Swangs

In Karyala, artists use different characters and performances to highlight economic and social issues, rather than following a regular storyline.

Sadhu ka Swang: This swang also imparts knowledge of scriptures. One of the important characters is *Maskhra*, who engages in conversations and asks questions to the hermits. Their interaction entertains the audience in a satirical manner.

Saheb ka Swang. Onc of the famous swangs in Karyala is based on anger towards the oppressive policies of the Britishers. The swang portrays the behavior of the Britishers towards Indians, providing glimpses of their interactions. Artists present it in a satirical way, offering both commentary and entertainment to the audience.

Bua ka Swang : This swang depicts a marriage ceremony where an angry aunty expresses her displeasure about her nephew's marriage. The swang highlights family relationships and the roles of daughters within the family, presenting the scenario in a humorous manner.

Seith ka Swang: The "Seith Ka Swang" conveys messages related to the practice of *Mahajani Pratha*, in which artists critically comment on the system.

Budhe kisan ka Swang: Swang presents a story that opposes polygamy.

Dau-Dayan ka Swang: In this Swang, the artists convey messages against superstitions and black magic. They educate people about the power of one's will and encourage them to rely on their own strength.

Bangale ka Swang: In this Swang, the artists motivate people to pursue education and highlight the drawbacks of an orthodox society.

Nepali ka Swang: In this Swang, the artist plays the character of a Nepali person, and it revolves around the theme of gender inequality, spreading the message of 'beti bachao' (save the girl child).

Coolie ka Swang: In this Swang, one artist plays the character of "Babuji" (an educated person from the city) and other artist play character of a *coolie.* The Swang is a satire and commentary on people who disregard the dignity of those from lower social classes and feel ashamed of doing manual labour.

Budhu ka Swang: Villagers are always curious about the various Swangs in Karyala. Artists deliberately use words with multiple meanings. In this Swang, an artist plays the role of a fool and entertains the villagers with their silly antics.

Each swang in Karyala disseminates a social message and also criticizes the prevalent evils in society. Rural Drama has the ability to entertain freely and also deliver important messages without hesitation. It understands its role as a social tool and knows that it can only survive by not just entertaining, but also by uplifting society Rural drama acknowledges its significance as a social instrument and recognizes that its survival relies on both entertaining and uplifting society. It is uniquely positioned to engage and captivate audiences in rural communities, reflecting their cultural traditions, values, and challenges. Through relatable characters, situations, and storytelling techniques, rural drama resonates deeply with its audience, forging a connection based on shared experiences.

Rural drama is not just about entertainment, it also tackles important social issues and teaches moral lessons. Through dramatic performances, it raises awareness about problems in society and promotes positive change. By doing this, rural drama aims to make society better and improve people's lives.

Audience Involvement in Karyala

Audience involvement is evident through the laughter of the people. Their participation can be observed through the offering of *Bail* (money) to the talented *Karyalchies*. Announcements are made in the form of couplets, stating the name of the person and the amount donated, which is followed by the artists expressing their gratitude and wishing for their continued prosperity.

Artists and folks

Glimpses of swangs in karyala

Swangs in Karyala are closely connected to society and provide artists with the freedom to add dialogues. They portray swangs that reflect the everyday life of the people.

Starting of *Karyala* with *Pujan*

***Chandravali* dance**

***Chandravali* dance**

Arrival of *Sadhu*

Sadhu ka swang

Karyala in action

Sadhu-babu ka swang

Amusing performances

Comical act by artists

Nepali ka swang

Man adorned in woman dress

Audience, artists and musicians

Entertainment by dancing and singing

Chapter -5

Conclusion

In the research journey of exploring the folk theatre Karyala of Himachal Pradesh, numerous interesting facts and insights have been revealed, shedding light on this ancient art form. Karyala is performed without a script and serves as a true reflection of social evils, culture, and mythological and anthropological dimensions for the native people of a particular area. However, in the modern world, this folk theatre is gradually fading into the past and losing public attention. Nonetheless, Karyala remains prevalent in Solan, Shimla, and Sirmour districts, serving as a main source of entertainment in rural areas since time immemorial. This impromptu theatre form of Karyala does not require a stage and can be performed at any open place, preferably at night.

This folk theatre is mostly organized by native people to fulfil wishes, desires, or *mannat* for the deity. Karyala, as a folk theatre, has retained its significance since ancient times. It is evident that this theatre encompasses a fusion of music, dance, drama, versification, and authoritative dialogues, aiming to sensitize, spread awareness, or simply entertain the people. Karyala is basically a theatrical art form that is performed without a script, devoid of grammar or literature, and nurtured solely through oral sources by the artists. It is an impromptu presentation that serves as both an educative and informative medium. Karyala acts as a source of entertainment for rural folks who are otherwise occupied with their daily chores during the day.

Karyala is predominantly organized in villages by the people to celebrate the fulfillment of their wishes. Himachal Pradesh, known as *Dev Bhoomi* or the Land of the Gods, aligns with Karyala as it is connected to *Dev Parampara* and incorporates various mythological characters. Over time, the storylines of Karyala acts have evolved, introducing new swangs with messages that are relevant to the present scenario. In conclusion, Karyala folk theatre serves as an exceptional mode of communication for addressing social rituals and emotional needs within rural communities. It not only entertains the rural folks but also plays a crucial role in sensitizing people about various social issues.

It is essential to acknowledge the remarkable essence of Karyala's artists, who, despite lacking formal training, possess a natural talent that has been honed over time. Their presence of mind and innate abilities shine through as they engage with villagers in an enchanting, informative, and artistic manner. Karyala is an unparalleled form of theatre that not only serves as entertainment but also holds religious and social significance. Karyala troupes effectively communicate social awareness messages, ideas, and government initiatives such as family planning, *beti bachao* (save the girl child), women empowerment, *nasha mukti* (anti-drug campaigns), and more.

Through various swangs, they disseminate messages related to social progress and transformation.

Karyala is a folk art that includes everyone, regardless of their caste, creed, or colour. It is regarded as a religious activity that promotes unity and brotherhood among all. Within Karyala, there are numerous swangs that incorporate a combination of dialogues, music, singing, mimicry, proverbs, poetic couplets, and humour. Each swang carries a social message within it. Over time, new swangs are added, keeping the art form relevant and evolving. Karyala is also economically feasible for villagers as it requires minimal financial resources. There is no need for a stage, and the performance can take place in an accessible arena for the audience.

Karyala folk theatre plays a vital role in building a strong cultural identity. It serves as a social tool that can contribute to rural development as well as individual growth. In Karyala, the connection between the audience and the artists is immediate and direct. One of the significant advantages is the absence of a language barrier, which often hinders effective communication. Karyala's appeal lies in its ability to touch emotions rather than rely solely on intellect. It establishes a direct rapport with the audience as it presents new and local themes.

It has been observed that the folk theatre Karyala is gradually fading into oblivion, primarily due to a lack of interest, especially among the younger generation. In earlier times, Karyala performances served as the sole source of entertainment for the rural population. However, with the advancements in technology and the easy accessibility of various forms of entertainment at our fingertips, this traditional art form is losing its popularity and appeal.

In conclusion, as Karyala folk theatre is fading away from Himachali culture, it is important to take action to preserve it. To bring this traditional art form back to life, we need to consider some important suggestions. Supporting and recognizing senior artists through government assistance would not only honor their contributions but also serve as an encouragement for younger talents to engage in Karyala. Additionally, incorporating local traditions, language, and arts into the school curriculum would expose young people to this cultural heritage, fostering appreciation and understanding. To nurture the growth of new talents, providing financial assistance and dedicated training spaces to local artists is essential. Moreover, leveraging the power of social media platforms can significantly contribute to preserving Karyala by expanding its reach and introducing it to diverse audiences.

Bibliography

Books

Aggarwal, Vir.Bala.,& Gupta ,V.S.(2001). *Handbook of Journalism and Mass Communication*. New Delhi: Concept Publishing Company.

Ahluwalia, Kailash.(1995). *Karyala: An Impromptu Theatre of Himachal Pradesh*. New Delhi: Reliance publishing house.

Bandura, Albert.(1977). *Social learning Theory.* Standford University: Prentice-Hall.

Balokhra, Jag.Mohan.(2007).The Paradise Himachal Pradesh A Complete Book on Himalayan State. New Delhi: H.G. Publication.

Behra, Charan.Guru.(2008). *Appropriating folk Culture A Study of the post-Independence Indian Drama.* New Delhi: Authorspress.

Benegal, Som.(1968).*A panorama of theatre in India.* Bombay: Indian Council for Cultural Relation Popular Prakashan.

Bhattacharya, Vivek. Rajan.(1976).*Communication in global village.* New Delhi: Chetana Publisher.

Byrski,M.Christopher.(1974). *Concept of Ancient Indian Theatre.* New Delhi: Munishiram Manoharlal.

Clarke, Kenneth.W., & Clarke, Mary.W.(1966).*Introducing folklore.* United States of America: Rinehart and Winton.

Crooke, W.(1993). *Folklore of India.* New Delhi: Aryan Book International.

Dracott, Alice. Elizabeth.(1992).*Folk tales from the Himalayas.* Haryana: Vipin Jain for Vintage Books.

Elder, Joseph. W.(1978). Mass Culture in Historical and Contemporary India. In Apte. Mahadev.L (Eds.), *Mass Culture Language and Arts in India* (pp.10-28).Bombay: Popular Prakashan.

Dundes, Alan.(1965).*The Study of folklore.* USA: Prentice-Hall.

Dundes, Alan.(1980).Interpreting folklore. Bloomington: Indiana University Press.

Fortier, Mark.(2002).*Theory/Theatre An Introduction (2nd ed.)*. USA: Routledge.

Gordon, George.N.(1963). *The language of Communication*. New York: Hasting House Publishers.

Gargi, Balwant.(1991).*Folk Theatre of India*. Noida: Rupa.Co.

Hans, Ashok.(1986).*Karyala A Folk Theatrical Form of Himachal Pradesh*. Delhi: Sahitya Sahakar.

Koul, Lokesh.(2016).*Methodology of Educational Research.*New Delhi:Vikas Publishing House.

Kothari,C.R.(2007).*Research Methodology Methods & techniques*.Delhi: New Age International (P) Limited.

Kumar, Kevel.J.(1981).*Mass Communication in India. Bombay*: JAICO Publishing House.

Kumar, Umesh.,& Mishra, Ranghavendra.(2016). Traditional folk media in Himachal Pradesh.In Mishra. Raghavendra (Eds), *Traditional folk Media in India Practice& Relevance* (pp.181-189). Varanasi: Bharti Prakashan.

Kuppuswamy, B.(1976). *Communication and Social Development in India*. Delhi: Sterling Publisher

Lull, James.(1995).*Media, Communication Culture A Global Approach*. UK: Black well Publishers.

Mahajan, Kamlesh.(1990).*Communication and Society The Emerging Human Concerns*. New Delhi: Classical Publishing Company.

MacBride, Sean.(1980).*Many voices One world.* Paris: United Nations Educational, Scientific and Cultural Organisation.

Mason, Bim.(1992). *Street Theatre and other outdoor performance*. London and New York: Routledge.

Mathur, J.C.(1964).*Drama in Rural India.* Bombay: Asia Publishing House.

Mc Garry, K.J.(1972).*Mass Communication. London*: Clive Bingley.

Murphy, Robert.D.(1977). *Mass Communication and Human interaction.*USA: Houghton Mifflin.

Parmar, Shyam.(1975 2nd ed). *Traditional Folk Media in India.* New Delhi: Geka Books.

Punia,Deep.(1993). Social values in Folklore. Jaipur and New Delhi: Rawat Publication.

Rani, N.Usha.(1996). *Folk Media for Development*. Mysore: Karnataka Book Publishers.

Sarkar, Benoy .Kumar.(1972 1st ed.).*The folk element in hindu culture A Contribution to socio- religious studies in Hindu folk-Institutions*. London: Longmans.

Schramm, Wilbur.(1972).how communication works. In McGarry.K.J.(Eds.), *mass communication* (pp.17-25).London: Clive Bingley.

Sharma, S.C.(1990).Sociological Approach to Communication. In Mahajan. Kamlesh.(Eds.), *Communication and Society* (pp. 61-94). New Delhi: Classical Publishing Company.

Sharma, Manorma.(2004). *Folk India A Comprehensive Study of Indian Folk music and culture*. New Delhi: Sundeep Prakashan.

Sinha, Biswajit.(2004).*Encyclopaedia of Indian Theatre-6 Folk Theatre*. Delhi: Raj Publication.

Singh, Mian. Goverdhan. (1992). *Festivals, fairs and Customs of Himachal Pradesh.* New Delhi: Indus Publishing Company.

Singh, Mian. Goverdhan.(1988).*Himachal Pradesh history culture and economy*. Shimla: Minerva Book House.

Srivastava , Sahab.lal.(1974). *Folk Culture and oral Tradition (A Comparative Study of region in Rajasthan and Eastern U.P)*. New Delhi: Abhinav Publication.

Thakkar, Monika.(2017).*Folk theatre forms of Maharashtra Narratives and Audience Response A Critical Discourse*. New Delhi: New Bharatiya Book Corporation.

Thakur, M.R.(2006).*Folklore of Himachal Pradesh*. New Delhi: Indus Publishing Company.

Thakur, S.S.S.*Karyala folk theatre of Himachal Pradesh*. New Delhi: Sangeet Natak Akademi.

Varadpande, M.L.(1979).*Traditions of Indian Theatre*. New Delhi: Abhinav Publication.

Varadpande, M.L.(1989).Invitation to Indian Theatre. New Delhi: Arnold Publisher.

Vatsyayan, Kapila.(1980). *Traditional Indian theatre Multiple Streams*. New Delhi: National Book trust.

Verma,V.(2019).*Society and cultural richness of Himachal Pradesh.*Delhi:B.R. Publishing corporation.

Vilanilam,J.V.(1987). *Religious Communication in India.* Kerala: Kairali Books

Vyathit, Gautam.Sharma.(1984 1st ed). *Folklore of Himachal Pradesh.* New Delhi: National Book Trust.

Journals

Bala, Kiran.(2013).Folk media can play a role in development.*Vidura*,5,61.

Bhardwaj, Harsh.(2016).Folk Theatre in India: Role, needs and challenges.*Worldreader*,1,1-6. https://docplayer.net/60676945-Folk-theatre-in-india-role-needs-and-challenges.html

Das, Sheelita.(2013).Folk theatre- its relevance in development in India.*Commentary-8 Global Media Journal-Indian Edition,*1,1-6. https://www.caluniv.ac.in/global-mdia-journal/COMMENTARY-DEC%202013/Commentary_8_Sheelita_Das.pdf

Edinyang., and David, Sunday.(2016). The significance of social learning theories in the Teaching of social studies education. *International Journal of Sociology and Anthropology Research,*2,40-45. https://www.eajournals.org/wp-content/uploads/The-Significance-of-Social-Learning-Theories-in-the-Teaching-of-Social-Studies-Education.pdf

Garbbert,lisa.(2018).folkDrama.*Humanities,*7,2-11. https://www.researchgate.net/publication/322236982_Folk_Drama

Kanwar, Kusum.,& Maheshwari, Arti.(2017). Utilization of folk art as involving theatre in communication programme in India. *Proceeding of the 4th conference on*

Communication,Culture and Media Studies Yogyakarta,1-6. https://journal.uii.ac.id/CCCMS/article/view/9185/0

Kasturi, Suman.Kumar., &Vardhan, P.bobby.(2013).Theatre and Sociological Issues with reference to Contemporary India.*Commentary-8 Global Media Journal-Indian Edition*,2,1-11. https://www.caluniv.ac.in/global-mdia-journal/ARTICLE-DEC2013/Article_2_Suman_Kasturi_&_P_Bobby_Vardhan.pdf

Kumar,Deepak.(2015).Folk Theatre in India: Role, Needs and Challenges.*World Wide Journal of Multidisciplinary Research and Development*,2(9),49-51. http://wwjmrd.com/upload/folk-theatre-in-india-role-needs-and-challenges_1553261009.pdf

Kumar, Harish.(2006).Folk media and rural development. *Indian Media Studies Journal*, 1, 93-98. https://www.semanticscholar.org/paper/Folk-Media-and-Rural-Development-DR-Kumar/506efaa15a8319ba6d20e012e9fe82a098ddb515

Kodavath, Yathish.L.(2015).Traditional Media for rural development and effective communication.*Indian Journal of Applied Research*,5,19-21. https://www.worldwidejournals.com/indian-journal-of-applied-research-(IJAR)/recent_issues_pdf/2015/May/May_2015_1492500398__181.pdf

Kumar, Shailender.(2012).Role of Folk Media in National Building. *Voice of Research*, 1, 1-6. http://www.voiceofresearch.org/doc/v1_i2/v1_i2_16.pdf

Malhan,P.N.(1986).National media Policy.*Vidura*,1,1.

Mathiyazhagan, T.,Kaur, Jagiyot., Ravindhar,M &Devrani,G,P. (2015).Traditional Media of Communication. *International Journal of Social Science*,4,159-169.105958/2321-5771.2015.00011.3.

Patnaik, Bala. Bharti.(2016). Communication Perspective of folk formats in India. *International Journal of Management and Social Sciences Research Review*, 1, 192-195. http://ijmsrr.com/downloads/1611201633.pdf

Nag.Baishakhi.(2013). Role of Theatre and folk Media Promoting social Development.*global media Journal-Indian Edition,*4,1-23. https://www.caluniv.ac.in/global-mdia-journal/COMMENTARY-DEC%202013/Commentary_6_Baishakhi_Nag.pdf

Prasad, Neeru.(2013). Folk Media: An active media for Communication Campaigns in Digital Era. *Commentary-1 Global Media Journal- Edition*, 4, 1-13. https://www.caluniv.ac.in/global-mdia-journal/COMMENTARY-DEC%202013/Commentary_1_Neeru_Prasad.pdf

Sharma, Anshul.,& Singh, Namrata.(2015).Role of folk Media in rural development. *International Journal of Education and Science Research*, 2, 59-63. http://www.ijesrr.org/publication/19/IJESRR%20V-2-2-12%20E.pdf

Sharma, Sanjay.(2017).The folk theatre in Himachal Pradesh.http://hubpages.com/entertainment/The-folk-theatre-in-Himachal-Pradesh.

Shaika,Shahi.,lal,Ruhi.,Jonjua,Mehak.(2021).Sustainable Development Goal: Case Study of using folk media as a potent tool in India.*Journal of Contemporary Issues in Business and Government*,27,4426-4443. https://cibg.org.au/pdf_10530_3a08ded1a3e23b20fdd3a552e00defd9.html

Sultana, Naznin.(2017). Significance of folk theatre as Communication for Development in Indian Context. *Theatre Street Journal*, 1, 138-144. http://theatrestreetjournal.in/wp-content/uploads/2017/01/Significance-of-Folk-theatre-as-Communication-for-Development-in-Indian-Context-By-Naznin-Sultana.pdf

News Papers

Ahluwalia,Kailash.(2018,January 13).Karyala.Himachal Tribune,pp4

Manta,Dipender.(2020,Feburary1).Wester threat to Mandi Culture.Mandav Kala Manch working to popularise local tradition.Himachal Tribune,pp4

सन्दर्भ ग्रन्थ सूची :

पुस्तक

हाण्डा, ओमचन्द. (1988). पश्चिमी हिमालय की लोक कलाएं. नई दिल्ली : इण्डस पब्लिशिंग कम्पनी.

बंसल, परमानन्द. (2005). हिमाचली लोकनाट्य धाज्जा सांस्कृतिक तथा संगीतिक अध्ययन. दिल्ली : संजय प्रकाशन.

व्यथित, गौतम. शर्मा. (2007). हिमाचली ग्रामीण रंगमंच यात्रा. दिल्ली : राजभाषा प्रकाशन.

गौतम, खुशीराम. (1992). हिमाचल प्रदेश का लोक साहित्य सिरमौरी लोक साहित्य. शिमला : हिमाचल कला, संस्कृति एवं भाषा अकादमी.

ठाकुर, एम. आर. (1981). हिमाचल के लोकनाट्य और लोकानुरंजन. दिल्ली : हिमाचल पुस्तक भण्डार.

पत्रिकाएँ

आहलूवालिया, कैलाश. (1989). करियाला : कुछ प्रश्न. सोमसी, 61-65

शास्त्री, शशिकांत. (1983). हिमाचल लोकनाट्य स्वरूप एवं परम्परा. सोमसी, 32-35

आहलूवालिया, कैलाश. (1977). लोकनाट्य-परम्परा और सम्भावना. सोमसी, 27-30

ठाकुर, एम. आर. (1988). करियाला. सोमसी, 85-89

हाण्डा, ओमचन्द. (1975). हिमाचल का लोकनाट्य : करियाला. सोमसी, 25-29

शर्मा, एच. आनन्द. (2019). करियालची. सोमसी, 45-48

देव, अमर. (2017). लोकनाट्य की जीवंत मिसाल करियाला, बरलाज व धाज्जा. हिमप्रस्थ,

151-154

अरुण, नरेंद्र. (2008). हिमाचली लोकनाट्य विधाएं. हिमप्रस्थ, 18-23

अजनबी, नेमचन्द. (2005). लोकनाट्य व लोकानुरंजन. हिमप्रस्थ, 8-14

हंस, अशोक. (2005). करियाला. हिमप्रस्थ, 66-70

हंस, अशोक. (2004). करियाला : एक लोकरंगमंचीय रूप. हिमप्रस्थ, 13-15

ठाकुर, गौरी. शंकर. (1999). हिमाचली लोकनाट्य परम्परा में करियाला. हिमप्रस्थ, 3-7

ललित, सी.आर.बी. (1994). हिमाचल की लोकनाट्य परम्परा. हिमप्रस्थ, 5-7

समाचार पत्र

करियाला से दिया बेटी बचाओ का संदेश. (10 दिसम्बर 2018). अमर उजाला. पृष्ठ 5

राज, योग (19 दिसम्बर 2018). पारम्परिक लोकनाट्य करियाला के माध्यम से सामाजिक

कुरीतियों पर प्रहार. गिरिराज, पृष्ठ 7

Gallery

Connect with Publisher

Instagram: @wkrishind
Twitter: @wkrishind
Facebook: @wkrishind
Tumblr: @wkrishind
Telegram: @wkrishind

WhatsApp or Call: 09999568276
Email: contact@wkrishind.in
Website: www.wkrishind.in

www.ingramcontent.com/pod-product-compliance
Lightning Source LLC
La Vergne TN
LVHW022026051126
851858LV00004B/57